Just Call me Kate

*Other books in the
True Girl Series*

Just Call Me Kate

Dannah Gresh
author of True Girl

and Janet Mylin

Moody Publishers
CHICAGO

Interior design: JuliaRyan | www.DesignByJulia.com
Cover and illustrations: JuliaRyan | www.DesignByJulia.com
Some images: © 2008 JupiterImages.com

Printed by Color House Graphics in Grand Rapids, Michigan - 06/2019

We hope you like this book from Moody Publishers. We want to give you books that help you think and figure out what truth really looks like. If you liked this and want more information, you and/or your mom can go to www.moodypublishers.com or write to . . .

Moody Publishers
820 N. LaSalle Boulevard
Chicago, IL 60610

9 10

Printed in the United States of America

This book is for Lucy—
my strong little Peanut

Jm

CHAPTER 1

Kate Makes Her Mark

Zachary Donaldson. Zachary Donaldson. His name is like poetry or something.

As I lifted my pencil to the pink bathroom wall, I had a quick conversation with myself.

Maybe I shouldn't do this. But I need to do something to get his attention. The high school cheerleaders use our gym for practice sometimes when their gym is being used. So if one of those girls sees this, then Zachary's definitely going to find out about it since he's a football player, and that will be so perfect. And this isn't really graffiti since I'm doing it in pencil. It can totally just be erased. No big deal, right?

My hand was shaking as I began to write in huge letters "Z-A-C-H-A-R-Y D-O-N-A-L-D-S-O-N." I finished by surrounding his name with a big heart.

When the secretary's voice came through the speaker dismissing students to their buses, I jumped.

All right, Kate, I said to myself. *Let's hope this works!*

When I got home after school, my mom handed me a huge piece of homemade lemon meringue pie.

"Hi, Katie. How was school?"

"Mom, *please* try to call me Kate! I'm twelve years old now. Katie sounds like a little kid's name!"

She gave me a hug. "Honey, you've always been our little Katie and that's a pretty difficult thing to change."

I sighed. "I know. I know. Just please try. Okay, Mom?"

"Okay," she said. "So did anything interesting happen at school today?"

"**No**. Nope. Nothing different happened at all. I didn't do anything different or anything. Just the same old boring day of school I always have. I'm gonna go eat this in my room. See you later, Mom!" I bolted up to my room before she asked me anything else. I'm a terrible liar and if she kept probing, I would have ended up spilling everything about the bathroom wall.

It doesn't usually take me very long to do my homework, but my brain was totally spinning. It was hard to think about anything except Zachary and how he might react when he finds out what I did. I finally closed my social studies book when I smelled burgers cooking on the grill through my open bedroom window.

"Meow! Meow!" Sharkey, my cat, was curled up on my bed and wanted some attention. I stroked his long white fur and began telling him about what I did in school that morning. Sharkey's almost always on my bed. He weighs twenty-five pounds and doesn't move much. Just as I was explaining the part about drawing the heart around Zachary's name, I heard the front door slam and loud boy voices making their way into the kitchen. It was my brother, Pete, and his best friend, whose name happens to be . . . Zachary Donaldson.

Yes. I have a major crush on my seventeen-year-old brother's best friend.

After I gave Sharkey one more good scratch under his chin, I looked in the mirror and made sure my ponytails weren't crooked. Then I cleaned the smudges off my glasses with the bottom of my shirt and headed downstairs.

My brother and Zachary were going over that day's football practice.

"Dude! You so totally rocked the house when you threw that pass!" Zachary said.

"I heard *that*, Z-Dog! It was sa-weet!" my brother agreed.

They speak in kind of a different language. I pretty much get it, which is good because sometimes my parents need an interpreter.

"Hey, Pete. Hey, Zachary." I blushed as they both gave my ponytails a tug when I walked by them.

"Hey, little sis," said Pete.

"Whussup, Kate the Great?" Zachary said. It's so cool that he and Pete both call me Kate, not Katie or my full name, Kaitlin. When I become president of the United States, I plan to go by Kaitlin, but not now. I'm saving it.

I grabbed some soda and opened it, trying to be chill, like I didn't care if they were there.

Pete turned back to Zachary and said, "Dude! I'm totally stoked for the game on Friday! If we beat Grant High that would be off the hook!"

Pete is the star quarterback for the Marion Sharks. I don't understand everything about football, but I do know that my brother pretty much rocks. It's mainly because of him that the team was undefeated last season.

"Yo, Pete," said Zachary, "I was wondering if I could just hang here this weekend. The fam's got a thing they're doing and I just wanna get out, if that's cool with you."

You would think that since my dad's a pastor, people wouldn't want to hang out at our house or something. But that's definitely not true. Our friends always want to come over—especially Zachary. He's been spending the night at our house a lot lately. Mom says it's because Mr. and Mrs.

Donaldson need lots of time to talk, but I'm **positive** it's because he likes playing video games with me.

"Whatever, man. My casa is your casa, right?" said Pete.

They high-fived. That's how they hug, I think.

Grabbing a couple bags of chips, a box of snack cakes, and a two-liter bottle of soda, they headed down to the basement to watch TV and stuff their faces, even though we were just about to eat dinner. I guess Mom has finally realized that nothing can possibly spoil Pete and Zachary's appetites. They eat 24/7. It's unbelievable.

When they were out of sight, I sat at the table and made a list in my head of all the things I like about Zachary:

He's the coolest guy on the planet.

He's kind of short and shaves his head.

He has this really goofy laugh that sounds a lot like a big, barking seal: "Arf! Arf! Arf!"

He wears his grandfather's dog-tags from World War II on a chain around his neck, which is so mature. (He is 17, after all.)

But the thing I like most about Zachary is that his left eye is brown and his right eye is blue. Sometimes when I'm sitting across from him at the dinner table I just look at his eyeballs while he slurps up spaghetti noodles and I wonder how they got that way. Mom says it's kind of like a birthmark, but I think it means he must have some kind of special power . . . like he can set things on fire just by looking at them. I seriously get a little freaked out when he just sits and stares at a game on TV. I don't want our TV to explode or anything.

I took another gulp of my drink and began tracing "ZACHARY" onto the side of the can with my finger. Who would be the very first person to notice Zachary's name on the bathroom wall?

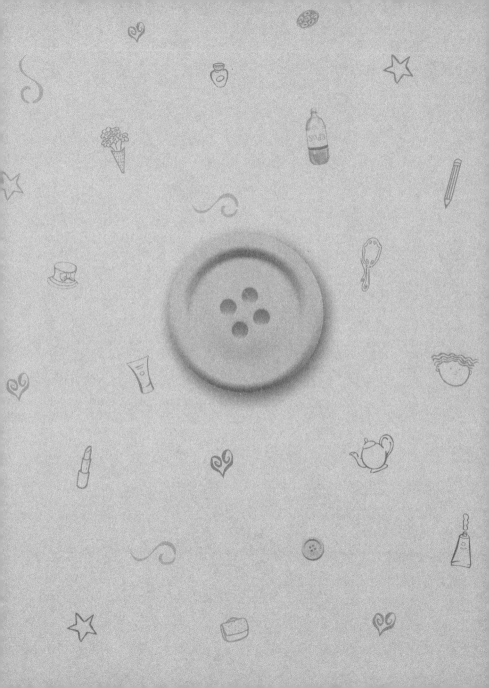

Just Call me Kate

CHAPTER 2

The most Embarrassing Thing EVER

As I was loading the dishwasher after dinner, my mom came in and said the ultimate weirdest thing she's ever said.

"Katie, I was thinking that we should go into town tonight and see about getting you a training bra."

I almost choked. "A **what**?"

"A training bra."

"What's it training for?" I carefully adjusted the plate I was loading.

"It's just a term used for a young girl's first bra," Mom answered.

"You want me to start wearing a *bra*? Have you *looked* at me lately? I definitely don't need one."

"Well, yes, but you're going to start changing soon and it would be good if you got used to wearing a bra. I thought you were excited about not being a little girl anymore," Mom said, moving her keys from one hand to the other.

"Sure I am, but I'm not into wearing all those straps and

buttons and things. I think it would feel like wearing a dog harness."

"Oh, honey." Mom smiled. "I think you'll be surprised at how comfortable and cute they can be. Now, start the dishwasher and we'll go."

"All right, fine," I said. "Hey, Mom?"

"Yes, honey?"

"Does Dad know?"

"Of course not, dear," she said with a smile.

"Cool."

Mom took me to the lingerie department of one of those big stores in the mall. Everywhere I looked I saw racks of bras, tables of underwear, and rows of nightgowns. A really tiny old lady with a long pointy nose and tiny black eyes came over to us. I kept thinking of how much she looked like a bird. In my head, I named her the Bird Lady.

"Can I help you two ladies find something?" the Bird Lady said in a high tweety voice.

Mom put her arm around my shoulder and said very proudly, "We're looking for a training bra for my daughter!"

I wanted to dive under a table and hide.

"Oh, how lovely!" said the Bird Lady. "What a spe[...]
time in your life, young lady! Come right over here. I think
you'll be very pleased with our delightful selection of starter
bras." This lady obviously loves bras.

When we first started looking, I didn't care very much.
But the more the Bird Lady showed us, the more I got
into it. Some of them were kind of cute. There was a
pink one with white polka dots on it that I tried on and
really liked.

We were actually having fun. My mom was digging
through the bras like she had struck gold or something.
She kept saying things like, "Oh, Katie, look at this one!"
or "Sweetie, I bet this one would be comfy!" and "Isn't
this one nice, Katie, with the lace around the edges?"

Then the most awful, horrible, terrible, humiliating,
embarrassing thing in the whole entire world happened.

My mom found a bra she really liked and held it up
high so the Bird Lady and I could see it. In a loud voice
she said, "Katie! This training bra is adorable! It even has a
little flower in the middle . . . oh, hello, Zachary!"

Zachary?! **Zachary?**

I turned to where she was looking and there he was,

walking past the bra section on his way to the sports equipment. Zachary Donaldson! I glanced at my mom, who was still holding the bra up like some kind of a flag.

"Oh, hey, Mrs. Harding. Hey, Kate-ster. Whussup?" He was looking right at me.

I didn't know what to do. My tongue felt puffy. So, I did the first thing that came to my mind. I dove under one of the tables of underwear and I hid.

The guy I'd boldly declared my love for on the bathroom wall saw me shopping for a training bra!

From under the table, I heard my mom say, "Well . . . um, Zachary, we'll see you at the game tomorrow night, okay?"

I heard Zachary answer. "Sure thing, Mrs. H." Then he said a little louder, "Uh, later, Kater!"

A second later my mom looked under the table, crawled under it, and sat beside me.

"Oh, Katie, I am so, so sorry. I should have realized . . ."

My eyes stung. I was close to bursting into tears.

Mom put her arms around me and pressed my head into her shoulder, and I totally **lost** it.

"Mom, I was so embarrassed! I didn't know what to do!" I sobbed.

Mom just held me and rubbed my back and said, "I know.
I know. It's okay."

When we finally came out from under the table, the
Bird Lady was standing there with her mouth hanging
open, holding a bunch of training bras.

My mom walked over to her and said, "We'll take this pink polka-dotted one and this one with the lace on it. Thank you for your help."

As we walked out of the store, Mom said, "Katie, remember what we used to do when you were little and had to get shots?"

"Yeah. If I was really good, you took me to get an ice cream sundae that was as big as my head," I said. I remembered how much I loved that, even though I could never eat the whole thing.

She put her hands on each side of my head and said, "So . . . I wonder if your head has gotten any bigger since then, because I could use some ice cream. What about you?"

"Totally, Mom."

The next morning I put on my new polka-dotted bra under a black T-shirt. Mom said I could only wear it under darker shirts so the polka dots don't show through. It wasn't like wearing a harness at all. By the time I got to the bathroom to check that no one had erased Zachary's name, I forgot I even had a bra on.

Lunch was kind of scary, though . . . and I'm not just talking about the food. So far I sit by myself at lunch. I don't mind so much.

After I opened my chocolate milk, I tried to identify the bumpy meat on my tray. Suddenly I got a funky feeling like something totally bad was about to happen. I lifted up my head and turned around to see Principal Butter staring in my direction. It was like one of those scenes in a movie where everything around me seemed foggy and silent except for Principal Butter's super-shiny bald head and heavy footsteps heading my way.

"Good afternoon, Kaitlin," he said.

I gulped. "Um . . . hey, Principal Butter." I had a feeling that now wasn't the best time to tell him I like to be called Kate.

"Are you enjoying your lunch today?" he asked.

I glanced down at the alien meat on my tray and lied, "Yeah. It's totally tasty and . . . um . . . nutritious."

Principal Butter bent his gleaming head down and looked at my notebook. It was open to a page where I had doodled Zachary's name all over the place in bright colors. He said, "Is this your notebook, Kaitlin?"

"Yes, sir. It's new."

"I see you've decorated it with the name 'Zachary.'" Principal Butter was looking right into my eyes with a little closed-mouth smile. I knew I was in trouble in a big way.

"Is Zachary's last name '*Donaldson*' by chance, Kaitlin?" he asked.

I looked at the notebook and stuttered my answer, "Um . . . y-yes . . . w-w-why?"

He straightened back up and said, "It seems that this Zachary Donaldson is a popular young man. Somebody wrote his name on the restroom wall. Isn't that interesting, Kaitlin?"

"Yes . . . it is," I said. I was beginning to feel really sick to my stomach.

He looked at my notebook again and said, "I'm sure we'll be talking again very soon, won't we, Kaitlin?" And he walked off.

I knew I was going to be sick, so I darted to the nearest garbage can and **totally** tossed my cookies. Thank God cafeterias are so loud. I don't think anyone even noticed.

This was *not* part of the plan.

Did Principal Butter really *know* it was me?

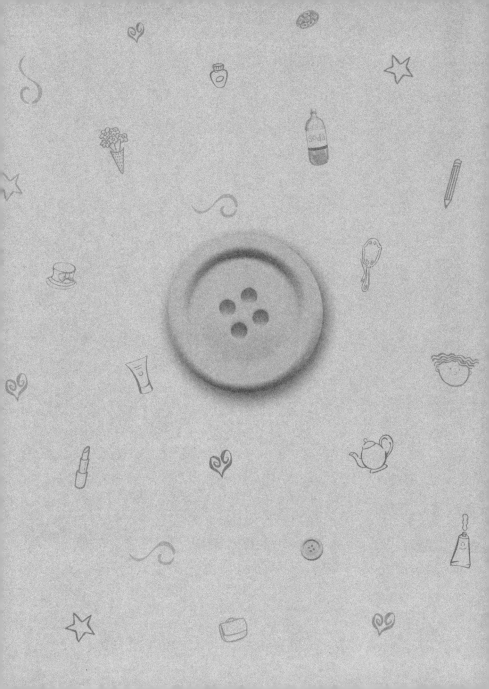

Just Call me Kate

CHAPTER 3

Why Do Bad Things Happen to Good Sixth Graders?

What if I get expelled and have to go to a juvenile detention center?! I'm pretty sure no president was ever kicked out of the sixth grade!

It wasn't surprising to hear Principal Butter's voice booming over the loudspeaker Monday morning, "Would Kaitlin Marie Harding please report to the office immediately? That's Kaitlin Marie Harding . . . report to the office immediately."

Everyone in my class was going, "Ooooo! Kate's in TROU-BLE!"

My teacher, Mr. Milton, who we figure to be about 110 years old, looked up from his desk with surprise on his face and said, "Kaitlin, you better go. Take your things with you . . . just in case."

Just in case of **what**? I thought.

As soon as I stepped into the office, Principal Butter handed me a big pink eraser and a pink slip. The pink slip said I had been given three nights of detention beginning this Wednesday after school. It had a place for my parents' signature. They were going to kill me.

I actually cried a little when I used the big eraser to remove Zachary's name from the bathroom wall. Just about the time I was done, the fire alarm went off in the school. We all got to go outside until the firemen made sure it wasn't really a fire. It was great to just lie back in the grass and look up at the clouds. One of the clouds looked a lot like Principal Butter. I'm pretty sure it was a rain cloud.

My mom's Crunchy Mexican Casserole is my most favorite meal ever, but it didn't taste the same that night because I was so nervous about giving my parents the pink slip.

While I was getting up the nerve to break the news, Dad said, "Katie, I thought that tonight I would take you on a little Daddy-Daughter date."

I just stared at him, completely freaked out.

Mom broke the silence. "That's a great idea! Go on and get ready, Katie."

In a fog, I went upstairs to change. I put on my lime-green baby-doll style dress with my pink leggings. And since I was having a not-so-great hair day, I stuck my denim newsboy hat on over my braids. I also wore the little pearl necklace my parents got me for my twelfth birthday. Maybe if Dad got upset about the detention he might see the necklace, remember how much he loves me, and forget all about being mad.

We had a good time over a piece of Triple Chocolate Fudge Cake. He put a big blob of icing on the end of his nose and pretended he didn't know it was there. He even left it there when the guy came to refill our drinks! Dad's pretty funny . . . I mean for a grown-up. But the whole time I kept thinking that I needed to tell him about detention. When we were done with the cake, I just blurted it out.

"Dad, I got detention for writing Zachary Donaldson's name on the bathroom wall," I said. I stared at the empty cake plate, hoping a tornado would come and take me to the Land of Oz.

"I know," he said. "Principal Butter called today and told me."

I looked up at him and said, "You do? Then why did you take me out for dessert if you knew what I did?" My eyes were starting to tear up.

"Katie, what you did was very wrong and I hope you'll never do something like that again, but I think I understand why you did it. I don't believe your intentions were to deface the school's property," he said.

"Definitely not, Dad! I just wanted to get Zachary's attention, and that's all I could think of to do. Now I see that it wasn't such a hot idea after all," I said. "So . . . what's my punishment going to be?"

"Your mom and I think detention is probably enough," he said. Then he reached across the table, grabbed my hand, and said, "Honey, you're a pretty incredible girl. If you just keep on being your incredible self, someday, when you're old enough, an incredible guy will find you and you'll have an incredible life together. But for now, just have fun being twelve."

"It's so majorly hard! Zachary's so amazing! He's like all I think about!" I told him.

Dad gave my hand a squeeze. I looked around hoping no one saw me holding hands with my dad. He said, "I know Zachary's great, but for now, why don't you let your dear old dad take you out on dates?"

"Dad, no offense, but you are so cheesy sometimes," I said, rolling my eyes.

When we got back home, a shiny BMW convertible was parked in our driveway. I walked in and saw Danika McAllister and her mom sitting in the living room. Danika's one of the most popular girls in school. We see each other sometimes and say "hi" and stuff, but we don't really hang out like we used to. Our moms have been good friends ever since we were babies. Sometimes her mom comes over to ask my mom for advice.

"Hey, Danika. Hi, Mrs. McAllister," I said.

My mom looked at me and said, "Sweetie, why don't you and Danika go in your room for a bit while we talk?"

"Sure. Come on, Danika," I said.

After I shut my bedroom door and turned some music on, we sat down on my blue fuzzy beanbag chairs and Danika told me she got a pink slip, too.

When she was throwing her lunch away, a container popped open and her mom's Purple Flurp dessert splashed all over Mrs. Hefty's face.

Mrs. Hefty is one of the cafeteria ladies and she's totally bizarre. The rumor around school is that Purple Flurp actually stained Mrs. Hefty's face blue. Danika told me that wasn't true.

"That's pretty bad," I said. "I wrote Zachary Donaldson's name on the bathroom wall, but I did it in pencil so it wouldn't really be graffiti."

"Wow. You're totally crushing on him, aren't you?" she asked.

"Totally. I just *know* we were meant to be together. It's like . . . destiny," I said with a sigh.

We both leaned back on the beanbags and stared up at the glow-in-the-dark planet stickers on my ceiling, wondering what we should do.

"Maybe if we had a club just for girls, we could promise not to let each other do stupid things anymore. It could be a club where we can totally trust each other because we won't blab everything to anyone else," she said.

"That could be cool. We could promise to be friends that really stick together and don't lie to each other and stuff," I agreed.

Danika got really wound up. She hopped up and announced, "We'll call it the True Girl Club!"

She remembered too. "Like that really cool show our moms took us to a couple years ago!"

When we were ten, our moms took us to a True Girl show in Cleveland. It's this crazy, fun thing just for girls our age. There were tons of balloons, loud music, and even a fashion show. We had a blast.

I hopped up and ran over to my dresser and pulled out a blue box. When I opened it, Danika squealed.

"Oh my goodness! You still have the friendship bracelets they gave us!" Her beautiful Asian eyes were all sparkly with excitement.

After sharing some good memories of what it was like to be friends before Danika got in with the popular crowd,

we knew we needed to protect our friendship in a girls' club . . .
the True Girl Club.

"Let's have our first club meeting this week," Danika
suggested.

"We have detention this week," I answered flatly.

"Oh, yeah," she remembered. Then sarcastically she
said, "Oh, boy!"

"A boy's what got me into trouble to begin with," I
reminded her.

I am really hoping the True Girl Club will help
me figure out all the crazy things I feel for Zachary
Donaldson. Only time will tell.

Just Call me Kate

CHAPTER 4

love lessons

Wednesday—my first day of detention. When people at school asked me if I was nervous about it, I was like, "Whatever" and "No big deal," but inside I was way panicky. What would it be like? Besides me and Danika, who else would be in there?

To keep my mind off going to detention, I spent a lot of time thinking about the True Girl Club. It was good to be friends with Danika again. Having a good bud could help me make some better choices. My idea to get Zachary to notice me was obviously a major disaster.

At the end of the school day, Mr. Milton told me to go to the Art Room for detention. Mrs. Hefty is normally the detention monitor, but she was taking the week off. So Mrs. Velasquez, the art teacher, was going to be our detention teacher, which was awesome. She's the youngest, coolest, prettiest teacher in our school. Even kids who don't like art love her class. She even lets us call her Mrs. V.

I walked into the art room and there she was, washing out some paintbrushes.

"Hi, Mrs. V," I said nervously.

"Good afternoon, Kaitlin. Oh wait, you like to be called 'Kate,' don't you? Good afternoon, *Kate*," she said as she signed my pink slip.

I relaxed a little and said, "Yeah. Thanks." I stood by her desk wondering what to do.

She must have noticed my awkwardness because she said, "I guess you can just sit anywhere."

After I sat down Danika came in and sat next to me. We both watched as Toni Diaz walked in. Toni's super cute and she's totally into sports. She said "hey" and took a seat. Next a girl came in that I didn't really know. Her family just moved to Marion. She gave a shy smile and sat in the back of the room. Mrs. V said her name is Yuzi.

Mrs. V went over a few rules and encouraged us to work or read. She didn't mind if we talked quietly. Then she sat down at her desk.

My pencil tip was broken so I walked up to the sharpener at the front of the room. While I was there, I scanned over the items on Mrs. V's desk: a jar full of paintbrushes, a carousel packed full of markers, stacks of sketchbooks, and a Barbie that had been painted green with flower petals glued around its head. But the thing that really caught my eye was her wedding photo in an artsy-beaded frame.

"Mrs. V, when did you get married?" I asked.

"Three years ago. Why?" she said.

"How did you know you were in love?" I asked.

35

She took a deep breath and said, "Well, let's see. Donny and I were good friends for quite awhile. And one day while we were laughing and sharing a bag of animal crackers, I knew I wanted to laugh with him for the rest of my life. It was like this natural, easy thing. I could just be myself and he loved me."

I sighed and said, "Oh."

"Do you think *you're* in love with someone, Kate?" she asked.

"I don't know. I just have this boy bud who's really cool and I'm in here because I wrote his name on the bathroom wall hoping somehow it would get his attention. I know I shouldn't obsess about him, but I just can't help it!"

Mrs. V was quiet for a second and then said, "Maybe instead of writing your thoughts on the bathroom wall, you could put your pencil to better use."

I didn't understand. "What do you mean?" I asked.

She said, "I think I can help you get over your boy craziness with a little bit of writing."

"What kind of writing?" I asked.

She opened her desk drawer and pulled out a plain green notebook. She handed it to me and said, "I want you to ask three people what true love is and write their answers in this journal. Then let me know what you come up with."

I took the notebook and held it to my chest and said, "That's a great idea, Mrs. V! Do you think it would be okay if I wrote other things in here, too?"

"Absolutely, Kate," she said with her amazing smile.

In that second I decided that she was a teacher we could totally trust.

"Mrs. V, Danika and I were talking about making better choices and stuff. And we figured that since we both got detention, we need to try and help each other out. So she came up with a great idea about a club. Wanna hear about it?" I asked.

"You bet," she said.

"Hey, Danika! Come up and tell Mrs. V about the True Girl Club!" I said excitedly.

"Shh," Mrs. V reminded, but she was smiling.

While Danika filled Mrs. V in on the details of the True Girl Club, I sat down and began writing in my journal.

37

Dear Diary,

What I'm about to write is a major big deal. This is my first official journal entry. I've never really kept an actual diary before, but I think this will be a great way to get all my thoughts and ideas all in one spot. Besides, when I become president, my journals will be worth a TON of money.

Mrs. Velasquez gave this journal to me with an assignment.

ASSIGNMENT: Ask 3 people what true love is.

Mrs. V's answer (not included in the 3): "It was a natural, easy thing. I could be myself and he loved me."

Danika called me back up to Mrs. V's desk and we all decided to ask Toni and Yuzi to be in the Club with us. They were really into it. Mrs. V even told us that we could have club meetings in her room on Wednesdays after school!

Walking out of detention with my new BFFs, I had a tingly feeling of excitement that started in my little piggy toe and traveled all the way up to the top of my ponytail, and it didn't have anything to do with Zachary. It was all about being a True Girl and the great new journal Mrs. V had given to me!

As I walked down the hall, I wondered who I should interview first to find out about true love.

Oh, yeah! I said under my breath. *I've got the perfect person.*

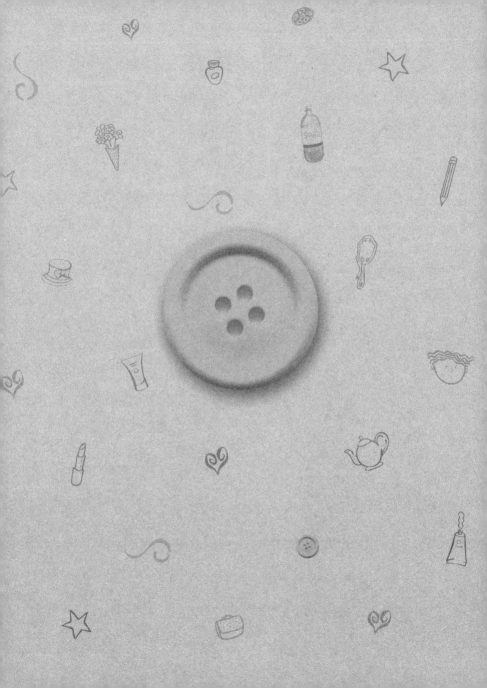

just call me kate

CHAPTER 5

Questions and Answers

Andrea Dorkelson. That's my sister's name since she married Barry Dorkelson this summer. They live in Malibu now, which **stinks**. California is so far away from Ohio. I figured I would give her a call and ask her my journal assignment question.

"Andrea DORKelson? This is your sister, Kate, who still has a normal last name," I said. I love making fun of her last name.

"Katie! I'm so glad you called! And you better be careful —you might end up with a strange last name someday, too!"

"Doubt it," I said. Besides, I already knew that someday my last name would probably be *Donaldson*. "Hey, my teacher gave me an assignment and I need your help with it."

"All right. What do you need?"

"My art teacher gave me a journal assignment when I was in detention today to ask three people . . . "

"*Detention*?!" Andrea interrupted me. "What in the world were you in detention for?"

"For defacing school property . . . so anyway, I need to ask three people—"

She interrupted me again. "Defacing school property?! Are you nuts?! You're only twelve!" Andrea was obviously confused, but I was too pumped about the assignment to fill her in.

"It's kind of a long story. *Please* just let me ask you the question," I said impatiently.

She was frustrated, but agreed to help me.

"Okay. Here goes. . . . What is true love?" I asked.

She answered right away. "We have a saying on our bedroom wall, '*You know you're in love when you can't fall asleep because reality is finally better than your dreams*.'"

"Andrea, no wonder your last name has the word *dork* in it, because that's like one of the dumbest things I've ever heard," I said.

"Come on, Katie! Dr. Seuss said it. Isn't that cool?" she said.

"Dr. *Seuss*?! As in the *Green Eggs and Ham* guy?" I was not impressed. Andrea used to be a total brainiac. She should know that a guy who writes kids' books wouldn't know anything about true love.

After I hung up the phone, I sat with my head in my hands for a little while. I got out my journal and wrote.

PERSON #1: Andrea's answer to "what is true love?" was totally lame, but I have to write it down anyway. It's a quote that says "You know you're in love when you can't fall asleep because reality is finally better than your dreams." What in the world is that supposed to mean? She used to be really smart.

NOTE TO MYSELF: Stay smart . . . even if you get married.

Pete was in the basement playing a football video game. Maybe he would have a good answer.

"Pete," I interrupted, "can you pause that for a sec so I can ask you something? It's kind of important."

"Yeah, hang on. Let me finish this play," he said as he tilted the controller back and forth. Then he started yelling at the screen, "Go! Go! Go! Go!!! Dude!! That was so righteous!!"

After he paused it, he turned to me and said, "So, whussup? Are you in need of my never-ending supply of wisdom, young Skywalker?"

I said, "Uh . . . sure . . . whatever. I just need you to answer a question for me, 'k?"

"Cool. What's the question?" He lifted his cup to take a drink.

I cleared my throat and said, "What is true love?"

Pete made kind of a choking sound and spit orange soda all over the place. "Yo! What kind of a messed-up question is that?"

"It's an assignment I have from school. Why are you so freaked out?"

"Well," he said, "it's just that the big 'L-word' is a totally off-the-wall thing. I don't think anyone really gets it, especially not me!"

"Can't you just please try to come up with an answer, Pete? I need to have *something* to write in my journal!" I had resorted to whining a little.

"Okay. Okay. Don't get all crazy on me," he said. "Just let me chill for a sec."

Just Call me Kate

He leaned forward and kept wringing his hands together. Then he took a deep breath and said, "I guess I've always thought true love will be one of the easiest things I'll do. Like I won't have to try to do it. So maybe my answer would be: If you're trying something and it's totally non-easy, then it's not the real thing. It's just you trying to make something work that wasn't meant to be."

There was a really long silence after he said that. We both kind of just watched each other. I don't know what *he* was thinking, but I couldn't believe my brother just said four sentences without saying "dude" or "sweet." This love thing must be really **serious**.

Back to my journal:

PERSON #2: Pete basically said he thinks true love is something that should be easy. My question is, if it's so easy, why did he spit his soda all over the place when I asked him about it?

NOTE TO MYSELF: There must be some kind of a secret about love that no one's telling me.

I had one more person to ask. I decided to IM Danika. Since she's my new BFF and the official founder of the True Girl Club, I figured we should start asking each other important things. I love Danika's screen name: *TeenyPopGirl*. She always wins some new title at the Miss Teeny Pop contest at our town's annual Popcorn Festival.

FuturePrez: can u talk?
TeenyPopGirl: ok whussup?
Future Prez: wut do u think tru luv is?
TeenyPopGirl: idk . . . I guess if u put ur hand over ur heart and say a boy's name and ur heart beats faster, then u luv him
FuturePrez: cool
TeenyPopGirl: gtg cu L8R
FuturePrez: CU

PERSON #3: Finally something that makes sense! Danika said that I should put my hand over my heart. If my heart beats faster when I say a boy's name, that means it's true love. I'm gonna try it now.

I went upstairs and lay on my bed beside Sharkey. I took a deep breath and put my hand over where my heart is. I said "Zachary Donaldson" very slowly and seriously and waited.

It worked! My pulse was faster when I said Zachary's name!!! I was in love! I knew it! I got up and danced around the room singing into my hairbrush, "I'm so totally in love! I'm so totally in lo-o-o-ve!"

47

The next morning before homeroom, I ran to the art room. "Mrs. V! Mrs. V! I have to show you my journal!" After she read my journal entries, I told her that I was definitely in love with Zachary because of the heartbeat test.

Mrs. V looked like she was really thinking about something.

She said, "These are some interesting answers, Kate. You've done a good job with the assignment. Now let's do another test, okay?"

"Okay," I said.

"What's your favorite food?" she asked.

That's easy. "My mom's *Crunchy Mexican Casserole*."

"Okay. Put your hand over your heart and say 'Crunchy Mexican Casserole.'"

I thought that was pretty strange but I did it anyway.

"Is anything happening, Kate?" Mrs. V asked.

I dropped my hand down to my side and quietly said, "Yeah. My heart started beating faster. I guess Danika's test isn't a good way of telling what true love is."

Major bummer.

She put her hand on my shoulder and said, "Do you want another journal assignment?"

"Sure. Why not?" I sighed.

"The first part of the assignment is to write a list of the five most important things in your life. I'll give you the second part when you're done with the list," she said.

I didn't see how a list was going to help me figure things out with Zachary, but what did I have to lose?

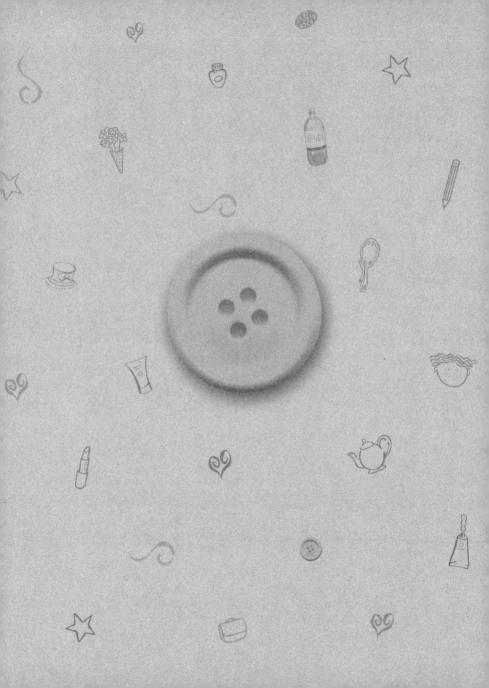

just call me kate

CHAPTER 6

Muffins, Pom-Poms, and Barking Seals

   That night I put on my striped hoodie and headed out to the garage. My dad was under the car fixing something.

   I flipped a bucket upside down and sat on it. "Dad?" I said. "Can you hear me?"

   "Sure! Just keep talking loud," he called out from under the car. "What's on your mind?"

   "Did you ever make a list of what's most important to you?" I said.

   "I don't know as I've ever made an official list or anything, but I've thought about it," he said.

   "So, if you had to make a list, what would be on it?"

   "Well, I always try to keep God as my first priority. After that would come your mom and you kids. Then there would be things like my job, my hobbies, my friends . . . things like that."

   I couldn't believe what he just said. "*You have friends*?!"

   Dad laughed. "Of course I have friends, Katie! Who do you think I golf with or play pool with?"

"I don't know. I guess I just thought you did that kind of stuff because you had to, not because you had fun," I said.

Dad scooted out from under the car and smiled at me. He has a really big smile where all his teeth show and his greenish-gold eyes crinkle up. "You know, just because I'm an adult doesn't mean that I don't enjoy life."

He patted me on the head and started digging in his toolbox.

Dear Diary,

Mrs. V gave me another journal assignment. I guess since the last one didn't work, she wants to try again.

ASSIGNMENT: Make a list of the 5 most important things to me.

That's easy.
1. School
2. Books
3. TV
4. Family
5. My cat, Sharkey

Reading over my list, I had some thoughts. School was not the most important thing in my life, and TV's not more important than my family. Sharkey's the best, but not as important to me as becoming a horse trainer or president of the United States or going to Australia.

I scribbled it out. Maybe this was going to be harder than I thought.

Friday morning I woke up to the sound of my alarm and the scent of freshly baked blueberry muffins. Every once in a while, Mom likes to get up before everyone else and do things like that. I don't ever like getting up, even if it's *after* everyone else.

I started working on my list again while I ate my muffin.

1. My family and friends

2. My dreams: horse trainer, president, going to Australia

Throughout the day at school I tried to notice what I talked about the most. I figured that would be a good way to find out what's important to me.

Yuzi and I spent like twenty minutes talking about clothes and what we're allowed to wear and where we like to buy stuff. We also talked about our hair. She has a huge puff of black curly hair on the top of her head. She's super nice and so cute with her chocolatey-brown skin and dark eyes.

Another thing I talked about a lot is the new *Alayna Rayne* CD that's coming out soon. Alayna Rayne is a totally fab singer and an amazing actress. I'm dying to see her in concert sometime. My mom and dad are trying to get me tickets to her concert in Cleveland that's coming up, but it's not going too well. There's all these rumors going around that people are paying like thousands of dollars just to get a ticket, but I'm not sure I believe it.

I spent the rest of the day talking to myself about Zachary Donaldson. I went into the bathroom and stared at the space where I had written his name. Today was my last day of detention.

While I waited for the dismissal bell to ring, I finished my list.

1. My family and friends

2. My dreams: horse trainer, president, going to Australia

3. Zachary Donaldson

4. Hair and clothes

5. TV and music

Since all of the girls in detention are True Girls, Mrs. V said we should use detention as club time, even though our official meetings will begin next Wednesday. I decided to read my list out loud in detention so everyone could hear it. After I read it, I asked, "Well, is it good?"

Toni, Yuzi, and Danika all smiled and nodded their heads. Mrs. V smiled too and said, "Good job, Kate. Did you learn anything while you were doing this assignment?"

"I learned that my dad actually has *friends*," I said.

"Okay. Did you learn anything about yourself?" she asked.

"No. I don't think so. Was I supposed to?"

"Maybe and maybe not. Are you ready for the second part of this assignment?" Mrs. V asked.

"Yeah, but is this one gonna make more sense than the last two?" I said.

"Yes, eventually. I want you to write down what you *don't* like about Zachary Donaldson," she said.

I laughed right out loud. "Well that's going to be a blank page because I like everything about him!"

"That may be true, but I just want you to think about it the next time he comes over to hang out with your brother. If anything pops out at you, write it down, okay?"

"All right, but it seems kind of pointless."

"We'll see," she said.

Tonight Mom, Dad, and I went to Pete and Zachary's football game. The Sharks were playing some team that wore red and white. For halftime, the cheerleaders made a really tall pyramid with one girl on the very top. Once she got up there she started the S-H-A-R-K-S cheer. Out of nowhere, a huge black bird started flying in circles around the pyramid and landed on top of the girl's head. She went crazy and tried to shoo it away, but its claws were caught in her long blonde hair. It was so-o-o funny! The whole crowd was in tears laughing at all of the pecking, swatting, squawking, and screaming. Eventually the whole pyramid fell down into a huge pile of pom-poms, ribbons, and sneakers. In the midst of everything, the bird got untangled and flew away with a hair ribbon in its beak.

By the time we all got home after the game, someone had already posted a video of the whole thing online, so we brought it up and played it over and over. Zachary and Pete were in the locker room during halftime, so they totally cracked up when they saw the video.

It was then that I first realized something about Zachary that I don't like: His barking seal laugh.

"Arf! Arf! Arf! That's craziness, dude! Arf! Arf!" He kept laughing and talking. Every time he barked out another laugh the hair on my arms would stick up. It was suddenly the most annoying noise I've ever heard.

I escaped to my room and wrote in my journal.

Dear Diary,

Mrs. V gave me another special mission.

ASSIGNMENT: Write down things I DON'T like about Zachary Donaldson.

I totally, completely, majorly HATE his laugh! He sounds like he belongs in a zoo or something! I can't believe I used to think it was cute, because it's the exact opposite of cute! It makes me want to run out of the house screaming! Mrs. V said she wanted to laugh with her husband for the rest of her life. Zachary's laugh is the very LAST thing I would want to listen to for the rest of my life!

Wow. That's weird. Maybe Zachary isn't as perfect as I thought he was.

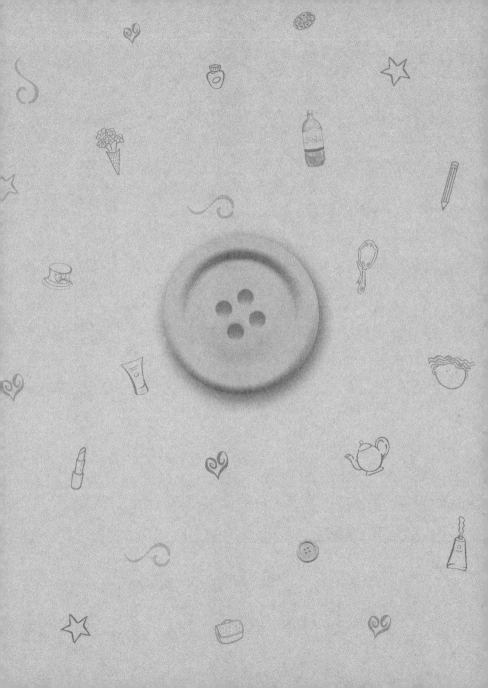

Just Call me Kate

CHAPTER 7

Reality Check

Over the weekend, I did my best *not* to make Zachary laugh.

I wanted to see if there was anything else about him that I didn't like. I used the Favorite Things list from my journal to ask him some questions. I felt like a detective.

"Zachary, did you hear that a horse in Bellevue had a baby with two heads?" I asked.

"Little dudette, horses are something I un-like. When I was a tyke, my aunt's horse stomped on my toe and broke it. I freaked out and haven't gone near a horse since," he said.

I dropped my carrot stick. "You mean, you don't like *horses*?"

"Totally not. In fact, there's maybe only one thing I hate more than horses," he said.

"Really? What's that?"

"Australia."

I almost **fell** off the barstool.

"How could you possibly hate a whole country?" I asked, trying to be calm.

"Yo, the way they talk makes my head flip," he said, moving his head to make it look like it was flipping. "And did you know most of the poisonous snakes in the world are in Australia? I *really* hate snakes. I wouldn't go to the Down Under if you gave me a million bucks!"

I felt like a balloon that was slowly losing its air. Did he really just say that?

This didn't look good, but I wanted to give Zachary one more chance.

"Your eighteenth birthday is coming up . . . have you thought about who you're gonna vote for?" I asked hopefully.

"I don't know, Kate-ster. I'll probably just do the eenie meenie minie moe thing and push whatever button I land on. I don't really care who our prez is. As long as the dude never makes football illegal, I'm cool! Hey, toss me a veggie, will ya?" he said.

I was suddenly filled with a desire to lunge across the counter, grab Zachary's neck, and start shaking him. Could this really be happening? Could he really hate *all* of the things I loved the most?

I slowly slid the carrots over to him and practically crawled to my room. This was major, so I hung my "Do Not Disturb" sign on the doorknob. I needed some **serious** time to write and think about what had just happened.

63

Dear Diary,

I feel like I'm on Mars and Zachary Donaldson is the alien. I found out that he hates horses and Australia! AND he totally doesn't care about the president of America! I can't believe I never knew this about him. I was so caught up in how he looked and how nice he is to me that I didn't know we don't even like the same things. Maybe it doesn't really matter, though. I mean, if we were exactly alike, that would be boring, right?

Our first official True Girl Club meeting was Wednesday. Danika is the club leader since the whole thing was her idea.

She had us start a list of club rules. So far we have:

1. Always keep each other's secrets.

   (We did say that we could tell our moms if we wanted to.)

2. No boys allowed.

3. We only wear banana berry flavored lip gloss.

Mrs. V basically just did her own work while we had our meeting. She offered advice a few times, but we didn't mind. It was great to be able to gab about all the stuff going on in our lives.

Yuzi's trying to figure out who really did pull the fire alarm last week. It's kind of fun trying to find clues and stuff . . . like a mystery.

Toni wants to play football with the boys but her parents are against it, so she's trying other things like band and stuff. I don't think that's going very well.

The popular girls have totally kicked Danika out of their group. It stinks to see how mean they are to her.

Yuzi thought we could figure out a way to put something in their shampoo bottles that would make all their hair fall out. It would be hard to be a popular Mean Girl if you're bald!

I filled them in on my discoveries about Zachary. They all thought it was crazy that someone could hate horses as much as he does.

Toni even said, "Sounds like your Dude is actually a Dud."

That kind of hurt my feelings, but I knew she was kind of right. It's beginning to feel like Zachary uses his head more for tackling than for thinking.

After school, I wrote in my journal again.

Dear Diary,

Our first True Girl Club meeting was the best! It's so great to have a place to say anything you want and know that no one's going to blab it to anyone else. At the end of the meeting Mrs. V gave me another journal assignment.

ASSIGNMENT: What is great about my family?

So far every time I try to do her assignments right away, it ends up being totally wrong, so this time I'm gonna watch my family, figure out why they're great, and THEN write it down.

When I went downstairs to watch TV, Mom and Dad were in the kitchen. Dad had his arms around Mom and she was giggling like a little kid or something. When I saw them, I immediately covered my eyes and said, "Oh, disgusting! Why do you guys have to do that?"

Mom said, "Oh, Katie, it's good that your dad and I hug each other."

"Whatever," I said. "It still makes me sick to my stomach."

I grabbed a banana on my way to the basement. There was a show on with a husband and wife talking. The woman said, "Why don't you hold my hand anymore?" The dude was like, "What's the big deal?" She was all like, "It makes me feel special when you hold my hand." Her guy obviously didn't get it.

That's pretty lame, I thought.

Before I went to bed I wrote in my journal:

One cool thing about my family is that my parents still hold hands and stuff, even though it totally grosses me out.

I looked at Sharkey and said, "I wonder if Zachary would ever let go of a football long enough to hold someone's hand."

Just Call me Kate

CHAPTER 8

Family Ties

Laney Douglas is one of the meanest, snobbiest people on the entire planet!

She's the most popular girl in school and she has decided to hate me. I think it's because Danika hangs out with me now. When I walked by Laney and her friends, they all pointed at me and started laughing. I went into the bathroom right away to see if my jeans were unzipped or something, but nothing was wrong. They were just trying to make me feel stupid.

Then she had Evan Lingle (who is cute I guess, but he's nothing compared to Zachary) come up to me and say, "Hey, Kate. Wanna be my girlfriend?" Then he waited a sec and said, "Oh, that's right! You're going to marry Zachary Donaldson!" and laughed. Laney and her Mean Girls were laughing, too.

But the worst thing Laney did was at lunch. It was tomato soup day. I was carrying my tray to the table and she walked by and "accidentally" stuck her foot out and tripped me. I fell completely flat on the floor and my tray shot up in the air, soup flying everywhere. It was really embarrassing, almost as bad as Zachary seeing me surrounded by training bras. But Danika, Yuzi, and Toni came over right away and helped me up. I love my True Girl sisters! I think Toni wanted to punch Laney right in the face. When I stood up, we all looked at Laney. She was crying her eyes out, because most of my tomato soup had splashed onto her expensive white capris! Even though I was still upset, I laughed pretty hard.

At dinner I was kind of bummed out and I guess everyone noticed, including Zachary, who seemed to be at our house more and more.

"Katie . . . um, I mean, *Kate*, do you want some more roast beef?" Mom asked.

"No, thanks," I said as I poked my fork in and out of my mashed potatoes.

"Honey, is everything okay?" Dad said.

My lip started to quiver and I burst into tears. I told them everything that happened with Laney, but I left out the part where Evan made fun of me for liking Zachary. "And I didn't even do anything except be friends with Danika!" I sobbed.

Pete was really miffed about it. "So this Laney person is being uncool to you and you didn't even do anything to her?!"

"Yeah," I said.

Zachary spoke up, "How could anyone be mean to the Kate-meister? Maybe she confused you with some crazy person."

I blushed to hear Zachary compliment me. He's so amazing.

"Zachary! Let's take the football team over to that chick's house just to scare her a little!" Pete said.

Zachary high-fived Pete and said, "Word up, my man! Let's do it!"

"Definitely *not*, boys," Dad said in his "I mean business" voice.

My parents then started telling me that I needed to keep doing the right thing and just try to ignore Laney. They also said I shouldn't be afraid to tell a teacher, but I don't want to do that. Then I would be a tattletale, which is *not* good for a sixth grader's reputation.

Just then the phone rang. Mom answered it and said, "Katie, it's for you."

"Hello?" I said.

"Roses are red, carnations are pink. You'll never get Zachary because you *stink*!" It was Laney's nasal, whiny voice.

I got mad. "What's your deal?! What did I ever do to you?! Leave me alone!"

She started yelling, "What makes you think you can be friends with someone like Danika McAllister? She's only using you to get back at us. You're too much of a loser to hang out with her!" I could hear girls laughing in the background.

I didn't know what to say.

Just then, Pete came over and grabbed the phone from my hand. Zachary stood beside me. He kind of smelled like cheese.

"You're Laney, right?" Pete said into the phone.

She must have said yes.

He started speaking really loudly. "Well, Laney, this is Pete Harding, Kate's brother. If you had a half a brain, you would definitely not be mean to my little sis! You may be some kind of a Miss Popular Chick right now, but I know a lot of people who can make your life rotten once you get into high school. So maybe instead of spending all your time trying to ruin someone else's life, why don't you take some time to *grow up* a little! Don't be hatin'! Start deflatin'!"

When Pete hung up the phone we all stared at him.

Then it started. My dad began chuckling a little. Then

Pete and Zachary started. Then me. Finally Mom joined in, and we all laughed until we were in tears. I ended up on the floor holding my gut because I was laughing so hard.

After we all regained control, Mom said, "You know, Pete, you might have been a little harsh."

Dad said, still laughing, "I think it was perfect!"

"Dude! That was crazy-awesome! It was like a scene in a movie! You totally went to bat for your sis! That rocks!" Zachary was majorly impressed.

I asked if I could be excused, but before I went upstairs, I gave Pete the biggest hug I've ever given him.

"Thanks, Pete. You're the **best**," I said.

"No problemo, little sis. Let me know if she gives you any more grief," he said.

Dear Diary,

Another thing that's great about my family is we stick up for each other, like Pete just did with Laney Douglas on the phone. I'm not sure Zachary ever gets the chance to stick up for his family since he's never home. He's been talking a lot lately about how amazing our family is. Maybe he doesn't hang out at our house all the time just because he likes to play video games with me.

School on Friday was a lot better. Laney wasn't mean at all. I think she even smiled at me once.

Toni was really impressed with what Pete said to Laney. Toni seems to like it when people are tough. I think she wants people to think she's super-tough, but I know she's super-sweet. I mean, she's definitely tougher than I am, but she's turning out to be a great friend, too.

"Hey, Toni, do you wanna come over to my house after the football game tonight?" I asked. Her brother plays football, too, so I figured she could just ride home with us. "Maybe you could even spend the night."

"That sounds cool. Sure," she said.

"Don't you have to ask your parents first?" I said.

"No. I'm kind of grounded, but since you're in the True Girl Club and your dad's a pastor, they'll probably be cool with it," Toni said.

"All right. There is just one thing we'll have to do, if it's okay with you," I explained. "My family has a movie night every once in a while where Mom makes a ton of popcorn and we all sit and watch something together. It's kind of like required, you know. Anyway, tonight's the night and since Zachary's going to be there, Mom said I could ask one of my friends, too. I know it's kind of cheesy to have to hang out with my family, but . . ."

"No, it's not." She cut me off. "It's cool. I wish my family did stuff like that. Sounds like fun . . . besides, popcorn rocks!"

75

We stayed up until like 3:00 in the morning talking and IMing Danika and Yuzi. When Toni was in the bathroom brushing her teeth, I pulled out my journal:

One more thing that's cool about my family is that we have Family Movie Night sometimes. Toni's family doesn't really do stuff together but she wishes they did.

NOTE TO MYSELF: Not every family is just like mine.

Tonight Zachary was with us, too, for movie night. It was the first time I ever hung out with him and I wasn't just thinking about being his girlfriend someday. I actually watched the movie.

It seems like every time I finish one of Mrs. V's journal assignments, I'm not thinking about Zachary as much. Maybe this journal really is helping me to not be so hung up on crushing on boys.

When Toni came out of the bathroom, she plopped down onto her sleeping bag and said, "Thanks for having me over, Kate. You're a good friend—a friend to the end!"

We linked pinkies and said it together, "Friends to the end!"

I had no idea that she and the other True Girl Club members were about to help me with my very last assignment from Mrs. V the next day.

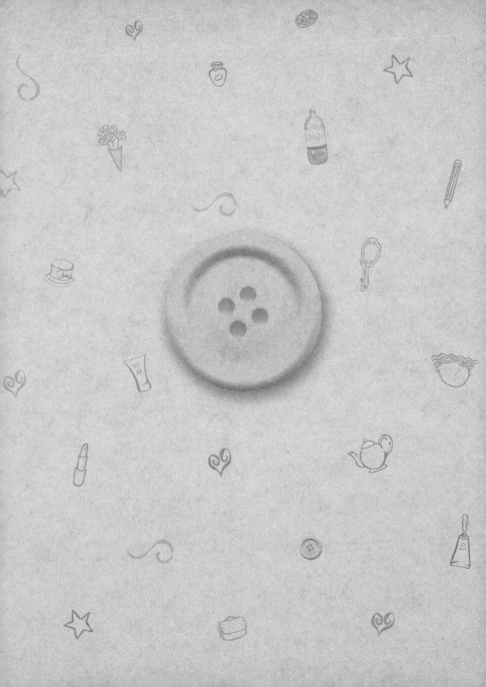

Just Call me Kate

CHAPTER 9

My New Favorite Number

"So, what do you think is great about being twelve years old?" I asked my True Girl Club girlfriends while we ate lunch.

Yuzi said, "What is the purpose of that question? Is it another assignment from Mrs. Velasquez?" She totally speaks like an adult sometimes.

"Yeah," I said. "I need five answers. I thought you guys could help me out."

"What does that have to do with your Zachary dilemma?" she asked.

"I'm not sure yet. It probably has something to do with 'embracing my youth.' So does anyone have any answers for me?" I said.

Danika answered right away. "I do. Being twelve is cool because you don't have to pay for lots of things because your parents do . . . like food, the house . . . stuff like that."

"That is pretty great. I hate it when my parents make me save my money for something. It takes forever," I said, knowing that Danika has never had to save up for anything in her life.

Yuzi said, "How about twelve-year-olds don't have jobs—especially jobs that move you all over the place."

"I've got one," Toni joined in. "When you're twelve, you can still have fun. Like, you can take a whole Saturday to play ball or something. The older you get, you don't get to have as much fun . . . you know, just to play around."

I thought of one. "I've always thought it's cool that I don't have to cook and stuff. My mom cooks the best food. I hope she cooks for me for the rest of my life."

Danika said, "Don't you think you'll have to cook when you get married someday?"

"I guess so. From watching my brother and Zachary, I'm pretty sure guys are only great at *eating* food, not *making* it. But I think if my husband and I live close enough to my parents, we could just go to their house every night for dinner, don't ya think?" I said.

"That's a good idea," she answered.

I wrote everyone's ideas down in my journal:

ASSIGNMENT: What's cool about being 12?

1. I don't have to pay for stuff.

2. I don't have a job.

3. I don't have to be boring yet.

4. I don't have to cook meals.

During our math quiz, I got my fifth answer.

Evan Lingle raised his hand at the beginning of the test and told Mr. Milton that his stomach hurt. This is something Evan does all the time to get out of taking tests. Mr. Milton told him he could go to the nurse as soon as he was done with the quiz.

About five seconds later, Evan barfed all over his desk. He sits kind of close to me, so it was pretty gross. After Mr. Milton took Evan to the nurse, he came back with Mr. Peeples, the janitor. I watched as Mr. Peeples sprinkled some orange powdery stuff around and cleaned everything up. I never realized how old he was before. I noticed that he only had seven little hairs on the top of his head. He also had ginormous earlobes. They kind of flapped around like elephant ears when he moved. I saw that his hands were really wrinkly and kind of baggy looking.

Since we had some time, I took out my journal and finished the assignment:

5. I don't have a bald head, gigantic flappy earlobes, and wrinkly skin.

At our next True Girl Club meeting, I read Mrs. V my list of great things about being twelve.

"I think you did a great job with all of the assignments, Kate," Mrs. V said.

"What do you mean? Aren't there any more?" I asked hopefully.

"Nope. That's it," she said.

"But I don't get it. What did they mean? Why did you have me do them?" I said impatiently.

"Kate, I wanted you to see that the very best thing you can do is enjoy who you are *right now*. There's plenty of time to grow up and have a boyfriend and all sorts of things. But *right now* you're an amazing twelve-year-old girl with a great family and great friends and big dreams. Don't you think so, girls?" she said as she turned toward the other three True Girls. They all nodded their head and agreed.

"I have to admit, I haven't been as 'Zachary crazy' lately. I guess I've been thinking more about my friends and stuff. It feels kind of good," I said.

Danika said, "Kate, you're so great just like you are. Zachary's cute and everything, but he's a ton older than you are and he'll be going to college next year. So, like, what's the point of obsessing about him all the time, ya know?"

Sometimes Danika makes a lot of sense. Since she isn't with the popular crowd anymore, she's not so stuck on herself. That's awesome.

"Fine, but if being twelve is so great and wonderful, why are some things so hard?" I asked. I felt a lump in my throat.

Mrs. V said, "Kate, can you go over there and pick up that pottery wheel and bring it over to me, please?"

"Are you serious? By myself?" I looked at her like she was crazy. "It's way too heavy!"

"Just try," she said.

I tried and it wouldn't budge.

"I can't, Mrs. V," I said.

"Okay," she said. "Girls, let's go over there and help Kate move that pottery wheel."

We all got around it and on the count of three, we lifted it up and moved it to the front of the room and set it down.

We were all kind of out of breath, even Toni. We smiled at each other. It made us all feel strong.

Mrs. V said, "Some things in life are kind of heavy. That's why we need to have friends like the True Girl Club to help us carry the weight sometimes."

"Mrs. V, sometimes you say things that I don't get at all, but I think I understand what you're saying this time," I said with a big smile.

Yuzi, Danika, and Toni all agreed. We ended up giving each other a big group hug. Toni had us all shout, "Go True Girls!" like football players do before a game.

We all had so much to gab about after that meeting, so we grabbed our stuff and headed out the door. Danika said that since her mom was taking us all home, she would ask her to stop for ice cream cones on the way.

We would definitely help Mrs. V move the pottery wheel back in the morning. Right now, we had chocolate chip cookie dough ice cream waiting for us! Yum-o!

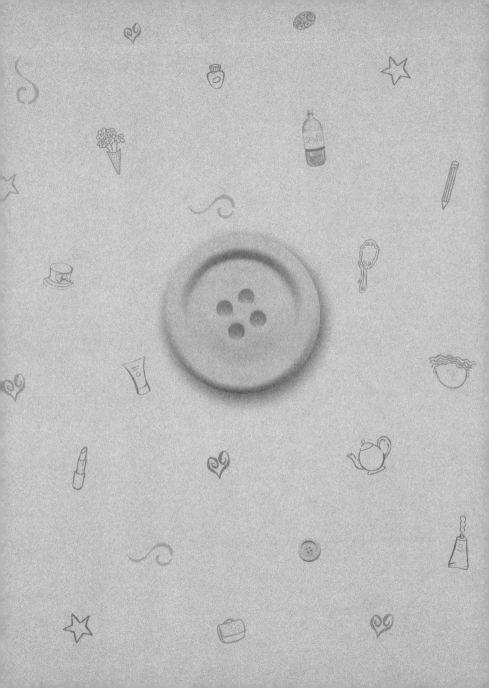

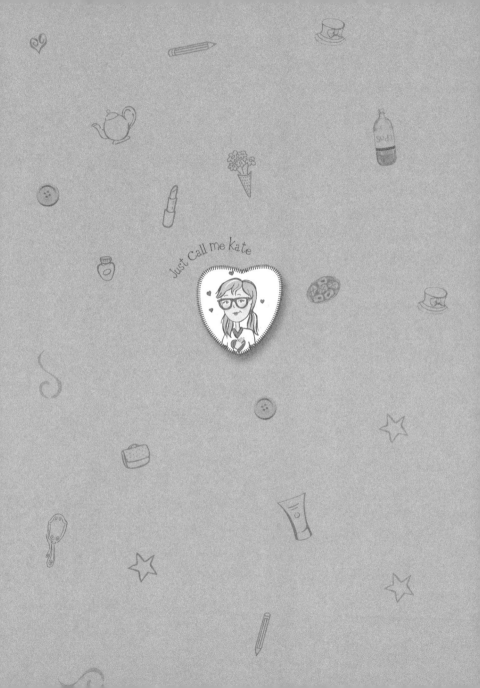

Just Call me kate

CHAPTER 10

Happy Me

Yuck. Homework in *every* subject?! I sat at the dining room table, surrounded by books. I dropped my head and landed facedown on my open notebook. Even though it was so close, I could see Zachary's name scribbled everywhere. Every time I looked at that notebook, all I could think about was Principal Butter standing over me at lunch the day before he gave me detention.

Mom walked by on her way to the kitchen to start getting dinner ready. "Hey, Mom," I called.

"Yes?" she answered.

"Can I get a new notebook?" I asked.

She came into the dining room. "But what's wrong with the one we just bought you before school?"

"Nothing, I guess. It's just that, I think maybe I shouldn't have written Zachary's name all through it. It's kind of . . . distracting sometimes," I said, looking up at her.

"Oh. Yes. I see. Well, I think I saw some on sale down at the store. I can pick one up for you tonight when I pick up my allergy medicine prescription, if you would like," she said.

"Really? That would be the best, Mom. Thanks!"

I stuck on my headphones and started with my science homework. It was all about earthworms. **Thrilling**.

I was listening to one of my Alayna Rayne CDs. I really hope I get an MP3 player of some kind for Christmas this year.

Mom says she likes to hear me sing, so I sing right out loud when I have my headphones on, even if she's close by.

"I've got to slow down, wa-a-y down.
This earth is spinnin' round and round,
Don't wanna miss this moment's sound
Gotta be who I am now;

Who I am right now."

I stopped and put down my book. The song was saying the same thing we just talked about with Mrs. V at the True Girl Club meeting! Crazy of all craziness! I put it on repeat and played it over and over while I did the rest of my homework. I was blown away by how fast I got everything done.

Zachary came over for dinner. Mom made this amazing buffalo chicken salad. Dad was telling us about some lady who asked him to do a funeral service for her poodle that died. As I listened to him, I was trying to get one of those little tomatoes on my fork. I kept stabbing at it and it kept rolling away from me. Finally, I took one more big stab and POP! I definitely hit it, but all the juice and seeds shot clear across the table and hit Zachary right in the eye! I stopped and stared at him, wondering what he would do.

As he wiped his blue eye with a napkin, he said, "Well, I think I've got another nickname for you, little dudette. 'Kate the Salad Plate!'" He picked up a huge piece of lettuce and threw it right at me. Since it was covered with blue cheese dressing, it stuck to my hair.

I blinked a couple of times and, without removing the lettuce from my head, I picked up my roll and hurled it as hard as I could at his chest. It hit him with a light thud.

A flurry of salad and bread followed. By the time Mom finally got us to stop, vegetables were everywhere except in the salad bowl.

A True Girl Series

It was pretty funny. It felt so good just to go crazy like that.

Pete said, "Whoa! Stop the planet, folks! I really wanted some more greenery for my meal tonight!"

Zachary said, "Well, dude, I've got some tasty spinach in my ear! You can have it, if you want it!" Then he and Pete started laughing pretty hard. Zachary's laugh didn't bother me as much. Maybe I can handle it in small doses.

Then Zachary said, "Kate-ster, you are definitely the coolest little sister I never had! For a sixth grader, you totally rock!" and he put his hand up for a high five.

I reached up and hit his hand and laughed, with his words ringing in my ears: "little sister I never had." Huh. So that's what he thinks of me. I'm like a little sister to him. *How come I'm not upset?*

Dear Diary,

Tonight after a food fight at dinner, Zachary basically said I'm like a little sister to him. I can't figure out why I'm not bawling my head off right now. I mean, like a week ago, I was doing everything I could to try and get him to see me as something different than

"Pete's kid sister," but now, I don't really care. Actually, it's kind of cool. Like Danika said, Zachary's probably going off to college next year, so what's the point of crushing on him? What's the point of crushing on anyone? It's not like I can go on dates or anything. Besides having another big brother might be kind of cool, right?

I stopped writing to rub Sharkey's head. He looked up at me and meowed.

Can I do this? Can I really be me and NOT be crazy over some boy? With the help of the True Girls and Mrs. V, I think I can.

I called Danika, Yuzi, and Toni to fill them in on everything that happened. They all told me how proud they are of me.

When I got to school the next morning, Yuzi came flying up to me waving a paper in her hand like a crazy person.

"Kate! Kate! You have to see this! You have to see what I have in my hand! Look! *Look!* I could be your campaign manager!" she said in a high-pitched, almost screaming voice.

I took the paper from her hand. It was a sign she had taken off the bulletin board.

Do YOU have what it takes to lead your class?
Run for CLASS PRESIDENT!

My mouth fell open and I sat down on the floor right there in the hallway. Yuzi sat beside me.

"This could be the perfect thing to get my mind off Zachary! You really think I could do this, Yuzi? You think I could be the sixth grade class president? Like, for *real?*" I asked.

She looked at me with her big brown eyes and said, "Absolutely, Kate. Or should I call you *President* Kate?"

I bet when I run for president of the United States someday, it will be really helpful if I was president of my sixth grade class.

Hmmm. Maybe it's time to start going by Kaitlin.

Run for Class President!

Girl Gab About Boy Craziness

Whoa! Kate was totally obsessing about Zachary Donaldson, wasn't she? But thanks to her True Girl Club girlfriends and Mrs. V, she learned a great lesson about her boy craziness. Let's dive in to the Bible together and find out some more!

"If I acted crazy,
I did it for God . . . Christ's love
has moved me to such extremes. His love
gets the first and last word
in everything we do."
2 Corinthians 5:13–14 (MSG)

Gab About It:

That is a totally heavy verse, isn't it? But I think it actually tells us a lot about girls obsessing over boys. **Answer these questions on the next pages** to see if you can figure out just what God can say to you about boy craziness through 2 Corinthians 5:13–14 (MSG).

❦ What does it mean that "Christ's love has the first and last word in everything we do?" ....
....
....
....

❦ Does God get to have a say in how we act about boys? ....
....
....
....

❦ How was Kate boy crazy over Zachary Donaldson? ....
....
....
....

❦ What did Kate do to help get her focus away from her crush and on to more important things? ....
....
....
....

💗 Have you ever completely obsessed over something or someone? ....
....
....
....

💗 What are some good things to do when you realize you're focusing more on boys than on the God who created those boys?..
....
....
....

PRAY IT OUT LOUD! One thing Kate learned is that her family is a really good thing and she needs to soak up all she can from her mom, dad, sister, and brother (and even her cat!). Wouldn't it be great if you and your mom or dad prayed about this boy-crazy thing together? Just talk to God like He's sitting across from you in a blue fuzzy beanbag chair. Tell your Heavenly Father you want to worship just Him and that you trust Him to take care of you now and forever.

Now . . . go clean your bathroom wall, True Girl!

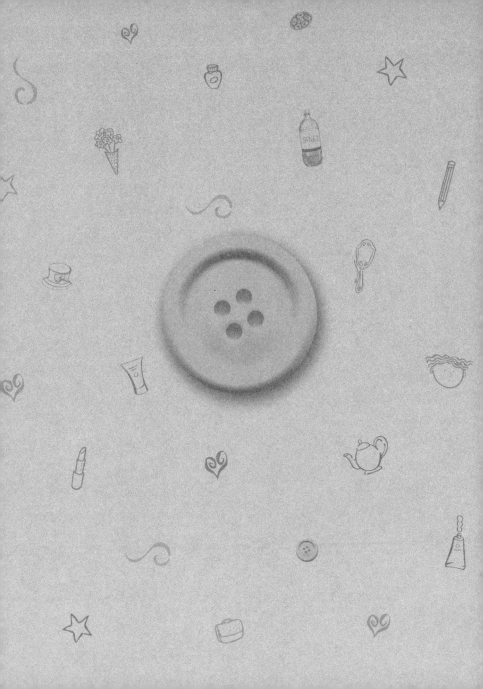

Just Call me Kate

978-0-8024-0645-3   978-0-8024-0642-2   978-0-8024-0644-6   978-0-8024-0643-9

Also available as eBooks

MOODY
Publishers®

From the Word to Life®

True Girl Series

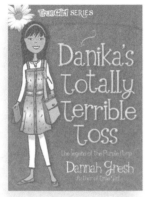

978-0-8024-8702-5

978-0-8024-8703-2

978-0-8024-8704-9

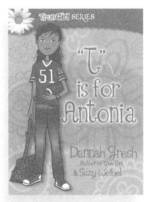

978-0-8024-8705-6

also available as eBooks

MOODY
Publishers®

From the Word to Life®

For more resources and events
for tween girls, go to

MYTRUEGIRL.COM